Feather Pillows

Rose Impey

Illustrated by
Robin Bell Corfield

PictureLions
An Imprint of HarperCollinsPublishers

Feather Pillows

To Graham,
in memory of Dora
RI

For the staff and pupils
at Great Dalby Primary School,
Leicestershire
RBC

Robin Bell Corfield would like to thank the following people for their help in posing for characters in this book:
the pupils at Great Dalby Primary School, Mary and Helen Hulbert, Mark, Carole, Briony and Thomas Bendle,
Martin and Debbie Burke, Danielle Mayes, Pauline Hogg, and Sue Oliver and Ruth Corfield.

First published in hardback in Great Britain by HarperCollins Publishers Ltd in 1997
First published in Picture Lions in 1998
1 3 5 7 9 10 8 6 4 2
ISBN: 0 00 664531-3

Picture Lions is an imprint of the Children's Division, part of HarperCollins Publishers Ltd.
Text copyright © Rose Impey 1997
Illustrations copyright © Robin Bell Corfield 1997
The author and illustrator assert the moral right to be
identified as the author and illustrator of the work.
A CIP catalogue record for this title is available from the British Library.

Printed and bound in Singapore by Imago

Sarah was bored with the adults talk-talk-talking.

They'd been sitting round the table ever since dinner finished, Mum and Dad and Grandpa and Uncle Alan and Auntie Sissie – talking and laughing and crying.

It was all right for Jake; he was being amused. They were passing him round like a parcel. But Sarah was a big girl; she was expected to amuse herself.

She had enjoyed it at first
when Mum suggested getting
out the photos. There were
lots of Mum and Auntie Sissie
when they were little;
sometimes she couldn't tell
which was which.

Sarah's favourite was the one of them paddling in a duck-pond, with their dresses tucked in their knickers.

And Sarah had enjoyed seeing the photos of Grandma Dora, especially the one of Grandma holding her when she was a tiny baby. Sarah was crying so hard, her face was screwed up like a little walnut, but Grandma was looking at her as if she was the most beautiful baby in the world.

Sarah had enjoyed the stories too, especially the one about how untidy Mum was when she was a girl. Once Grandma had got so cross with her that she'd opened the bedroom window and thrown all Mum's clothes onto the front lawn, just as Mum was walking home from school with her friends.

But now everyone was starting to get sad and talk about Grandma's illness which made Sarah remember that Grandma Dora had died and wasn't just away somewhere visiting, as she sometimes liked to think she was.

Sarah tugged at Mum's sleeve for attention.

"Why don't you go and play in the garden, Sweetie," said Mum.

"No one to play with,"
Sarah grumbled.

"Take Jake," said Dad.

Uncle Alan stood Jake on the floor.

"All right," said Sarah. "Come on."

She led Jake down the six steps into Grandpa's garden.

On the last step Jake sat down with a bump and picked up an empty snail shell. He poked his finger inside as far as it would go. Sarah took the shell away from him.

"Stop that, Jake," she said, "it's dirty. You'll catch germs if you're not careful."

Sarah led Jake across the lawn, into the shade of an apple tree.

Jake started to pull at his shoes.

"No, leave them on," she told him. "Look at this instead."

Sarah showed Jake the photo Grandpa had given her of Grandma in a deckchair with an ice-cream. There was a donkey's head appearing over Grandma's shoulder as if it was about to eat the cornet. It was taken on holiday, before Jake was born.

"This is your Grandma, I mean *was* your Grandma," she told him. Jake tried to take the photo but Sarah moved it away in case he creased it. She gave him a silver sweet wrapper out of her pocket instead; Jake put it straight into his mouth.

"Oh, no you don't," she said, sounding exactly like her mum.

Jake looked at her, puzzled for a moment. Sarah laughed
and pushed him onto his back and rolled him over and over

as if he was a rolling pin and she was rolling pastry.

Jake laughed too.

A blackbird landed close to them on the grass. Then Sarah
remembered Grandma playing 'two little dicky birds sitting
on a wall'. Grandma used to tear two little strips of newspaper
and wrap them round her fingers, wetting the ends to make
them stick. The way she made the birds appear and disappear
was like a magic trick. Sarah tried to do the trick, with pieces
of grass instead, but Jake got bored and crawled away from her
over the lawn.

At the end of the garden
was a little brick outbuilding.
Jake banged on the door and
rattled the handle, but nothing
happened.

"No use knocking," said
Sarah, "nobody lives there."

But Jake went on rattling
hopefully. Sarah gave the door
a push and Jake tumbled in
and burst out crying.
She tried to comfort
him, but Jake pushed
her away.

Inside the little house was a lawn-mower and a wheelbarrow, deckchairs and a couple of old bikes that Mum and Auntie Sissie used to ride. Jake tried to climb into the wheelbarrow. Sarah tugged his nappy and he rolled in and curled up, with his thumb in his mouth.

"You mustn't go to sleep," said Sarah. She pulled out his thumb, but Jake stuck it back in.

It was cool in the little house and quiet. The sun's rays came slantwise through the windows. Thousands of specks of dust quivered in the light, as if they were alive.

On the window-sill, Sarah spotted a tiny white feather. She picked it up and tickled herself on the end of her nose with it. She remembered a day, before Jake was born, when he was still in Mum's tummy, a hot day, just like this one.

Sarah and Mum and Grandma Dora came down to the little
house to make feather pillows out of Great Grandma's feather
bed. They were all wearing old clothes and scarves tied round
their hair, to keep the feathers out. Sarah wore an apron of
Grandma's with two pockets full of lavender.

When they cut open the feather bed, hundreds of tiny feathers
flew up in a cloud, getting up Sarah's nose and making it itch.
Mum and Grandma took handfuls and pushed them deep into
the pillowcases. Each time they called her,
Sarah came and sprinkled in handfuls
of lavender, to make the pillows
smell sweet.

When they were full, Mum and Grandma sat on stools and
sewed up the pillows, with tight little stitches to keep the feathers
in, while Sarah chased feathers out of the door, into the sunlight.

Sarah looked round at Jake, snoozing in the wheelbarrow. She stroked the inside of her arm with the feather. It tickled and made her laugh, even though there were two little tears running down her face. It felt funny, laughing and crying at the same time.

Suddenly, Sarah could feel eyes on her. In the doorway were Mum and Dad and Uncle Alan and Auntie Sissie, all watching her.

"I see Jake's asleep again," said Dad.

"What have you been doing?"
asked Mum.

"Thinking."

"Nice thoughts?" asked Dad.

Sarah nodded.

"So what's making you cry?"

"Feather pillows," said Sarah.

"Ahhh," said Mum.

And she scooped Sarah
up, as big as she was, and
hugged her very tight.
And Sarah tickled Mum's
nose with the feather and
they both laughed and cried,
at the same time.

The Thing That Bothered FARMER BROWN

by Teri Sloat

illustrated by Nadine Bernard Westcott

ORCHARD BOOKS

To my Farmer Brown, Robert,
and to light sleepers everywhere.
T. S.

For Sarah
and her barnful of animals.
N. B. W.

ORCHARD BOOKS
96 Leonard Street, London EC2A 4RH
Orchard Books Australia
14 Mars Road, Lane Cove, NSW 2066
First published in the United States
by Orchard Books, New York.
First published in Great Britain 1996
First paperback publication 1996
Text copyright © Teri Sloat 1995
Illustrations copyright © Nadine Bernard Westcott 1995
1 86039 220 2 (hardback)
1 86039 311 X (paperback)
A CIP catalogue record for this book
is available from the British Library.
Printed in Belgium.

"The animals are bedded down;
My chores are done," said Farmer Brown.
And as he stretched, the sun went down.

But tails and feathers swished the ground
At something flying round and round
With a tiny, whiny, humming sound.

The farmer ate his soup and bread,

Put his nightshirt on, and climbed into bed.
He pulled up the sheet and the worn-out spread
And, closing his eyes, he laid down his head.

But something bothered Farmer Brown;
Something was flying round and round
With a tiny, whiny, humming sound.

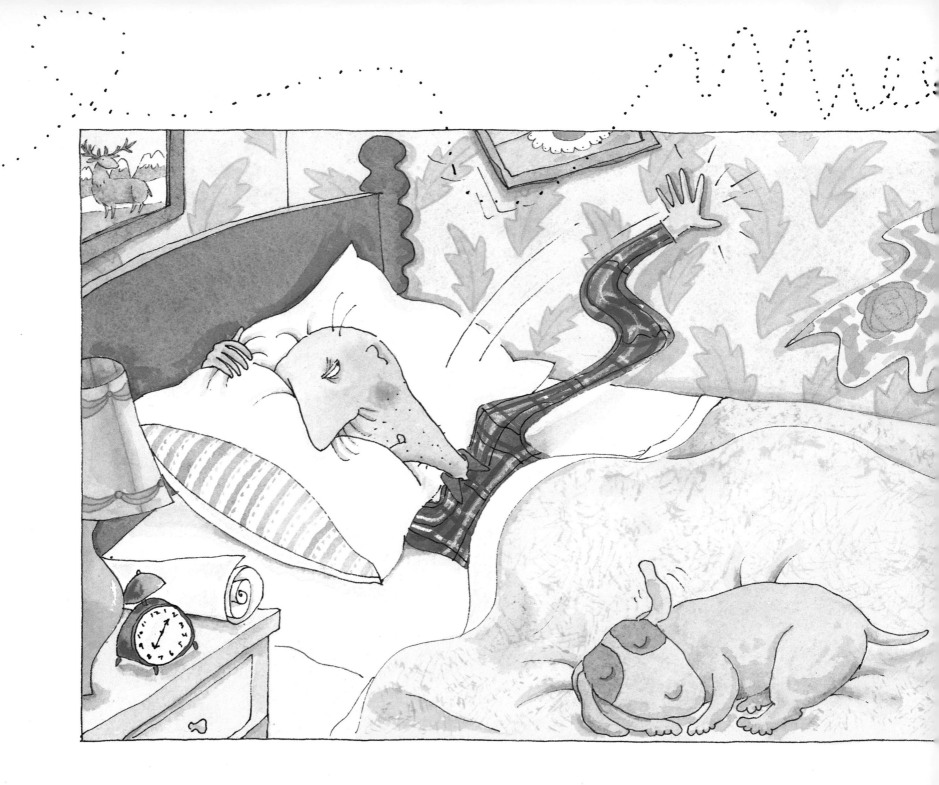

The farmer gave a SWAT at the wall

That roused the horse asleep in the stall
And the weary donkey, Butterball.
But it didn't stop the humming at all.

    The old horse neighed,
    The donkey brayed . . .

But the thing annoying Farmer Brown
Was something flying round and round
With a tiny, whiny, humming sound.

His newspaper hit the wall
With a WHACK

That upset the doves roosting in back
And the dairy cows marked white and black.
But the humming just kept coming back.

 The doves cooed,
 The cows mooed,
 The old horse neighed,
 The donkey brayed . . .

But the thing disturbing Farmer Brown
Was something flying round and round
With a tiny, whiny, humming sound.

The farmer gave a SNAP with his sheet

That startled the grumpy old goat to his feet
And made the hens flutter, scattering wheat.
But the humming barely missed a beat.

The old goat bucked,
The chickens clucked,
The doves cooed,
The cows mooed,
The old horse neighed,
The donkey brayed . . .

But the thing exhausting Farmer Brown
Was something flying round and round
With a tiny, whiny, humming sound.

This time he stood still
While the humming came near.
He lifted his hand as it lit on his ear,

Gave a SMACK
To his noggin' so loud and so clear
That the old dog and cat
Couldn't help overhear.

The cat yowled,
The dog howled,
The old goat bucked,
The chickens clucked,
The doves cooed,
The cows mooed,
The old horse neighed,
The donkey brayed . . .

But the farmer SNORED!

The animals slowly settled down
With heads tucked in and
Tails curled round.
The entire farm was sleeping sound

When they heard it flying round and round . . .

That tiny, whiny, humming sound.